For travellers everywhere...
and for Tom — for being my home.

A TEMPLAR BOOK

This edition first published in the UK in 2015 by Templar Publishing,
part of the Bonnier Publishing Group,
Deepdene Lodge, Deepdene Avenue, Dorking, Surrey, RH5 4AT, UK
www.templarco.co.uk
First Published in the U.S. in 2015 by Random House Children's Books.
Published by arrangement with Random House Children's Books,
a division of Random House LLC. New York, New York, U.S.A.

ISBN 978-1-78370-315-9 (hardback)
ISBN 978-1-78370-314-2 (paperback)

Design by Nicole de Las Heras

Printed in China

HOME TWEET HOME

words & pictures by
Courtney Dicmas

High up on a cliff
above the shimmering sea,
there lived a family of swallows.

There were ten brothers and sisters:

Edgar, Maude, Rupert, Helena, Winnie, Cecil
Beatrix, Rosalie...

Pippi and Burt.

Each night,
big brother Burt
looked at the moon
while big sister
Pippi worried.

"This nest is
too SMALL!"
Pippi grumbled.

"A bigger nest would have room for Rupert's stinky feet...

and Maude's judo...

and Cecil's band practice."

PHEEER ZWEE

"Well, the world is BIG and so are we," chirped Burt.

"Let's go and find somewhere BIG to live!"

So away they flew
into the night sky
to find a new place
to call home.

The next morning they found a spot that looked just right.

"This is PERFECT!" said Burt.
"It's BIG and sturdy! I wonder if we could
live here."

Suurre yoouu caaan !

AAAAH!

"OH! That is VERY kind of you!" said Pippi.
"But I think perhaps we're looking for something a bit, um, softer... "

The next time they were
more careful.

"This looks SO fluffy," sighed Pippi.

"I wonder if we could live... "

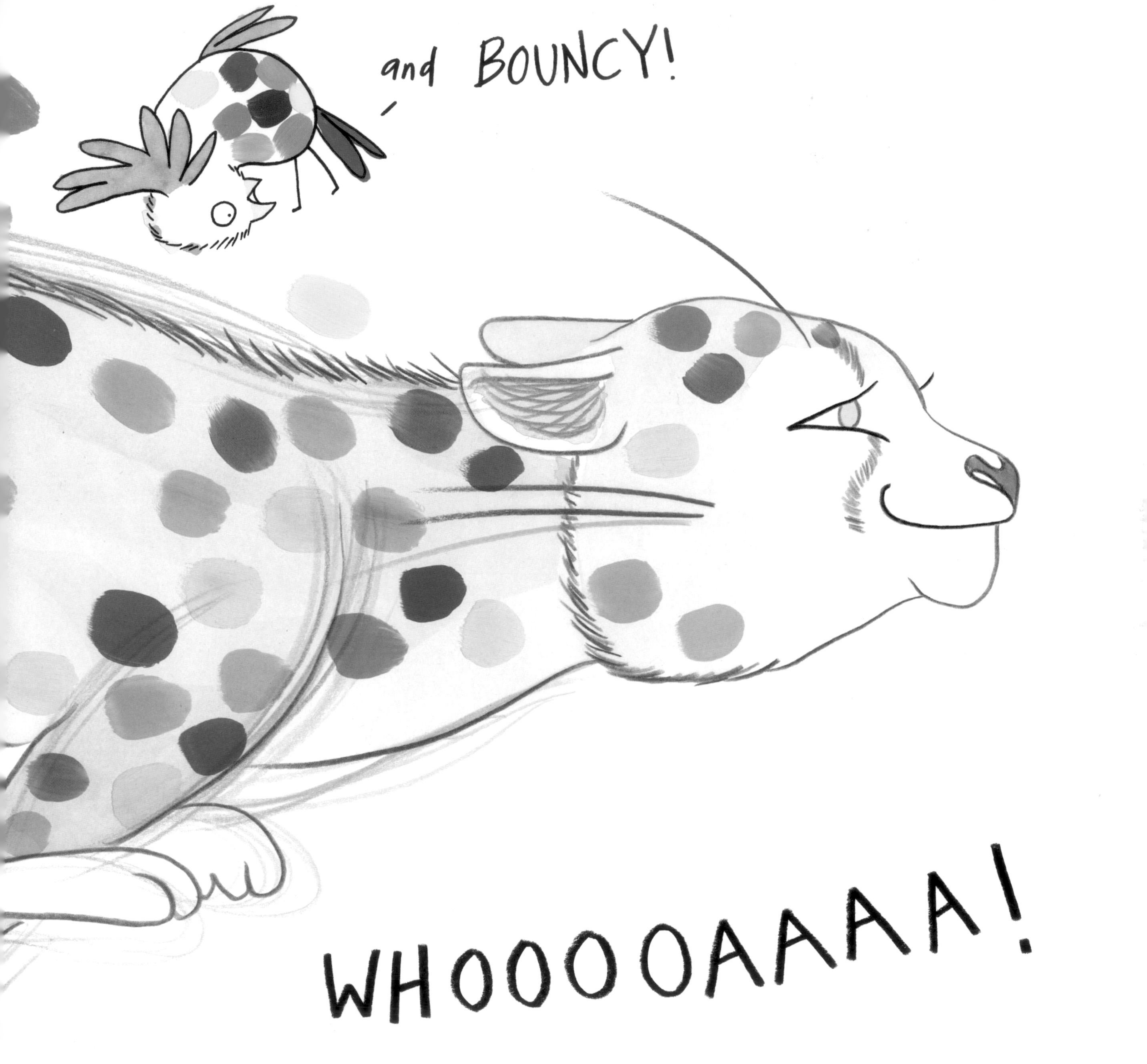
and BOUNCY!
WHOOOOAAAA!

"Phew! That was close,"
squeaked Pippi.
"We were almost lunch."

"Now, this looks PERFECT," chirped Burt.
"Not too hard, not too soft, and not too pointy."

"I've always wanted to live on an island!" said Pippi.

"This isn't what I thought it would be," sighed Burt.

"Can't we find somewhere that's not so big...

or squishy...

or hungry?"

"That's

"Burt, you're a GENIUS!"
said Pippi.

"I'm glad the world is so big,"
sighed Burt. "It makes coming home
so much better."

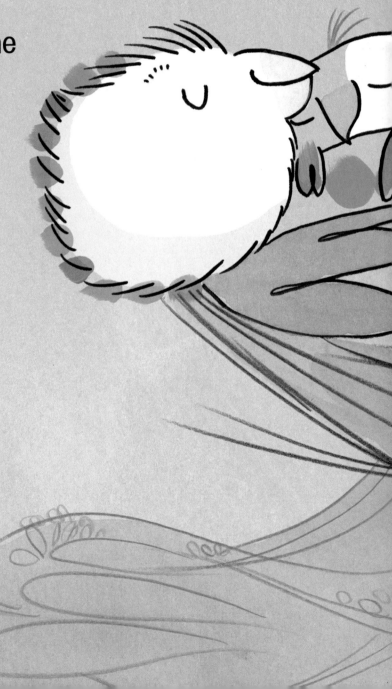